I0781188

Ground Zero

First printing April 2024

Library of Congress Cataloging-in-Publication Data

Naqvi, Sam
ground zero / dr. sam naqvi

Paperback ISBN: 978-1-965092-46-0
Hardcover ISBN: 978-1-965092-47-7

Published by AR PRESS, an American Real Publishing Company
Roger L. Brooks, Publisher
roger@incubatemedia.us
americanrealpublishing.com

Interior design by Eva Myrick, MSCP

Printed in the U.S.A.

UNFOLDING THE 2020 COVID-19 PANDEMIC

GROUND ZERO

DR. SAM'S JOURNEY: A WARRIOR'S TALE FROM THE FRONTLINES OF THE MEDICAL BATTLEFIELD

Dr. Sam Naqvi

...life was good and seemed to be cruising, but
I found myself up against an unseen
enemy where defeat meant a certain death, and
turning back was not an option. I must fight with
bare hands, and the cliff hanger began...

To my mother, Nargis Naqvi. The greatest storyteller I have ever known, the one who made me
believe that there is a writer in me.

Preface and Acknowledgments

Finally, *Ground Zero* takes off the ground. It was an incredible journey to write this book, and a kind of emotional roller coaster. A promise duly fulfilled. A promise that I made to myself and to my mother Nargis a long time ago. Walking down memory lane is very nostalgic and not as easy as it sounds. A long time ago during the long cold winter nights, a cuddly, young Sam, while listening to his mom's mind-blowing stories—literally out of this world—wouldn't have imagined that one day he would be telling his own story to the rest of the world. She instilled the grains of writing in my young mind and here I am paying her back with all my love. I must mention my brother Javed Naqvi, also nicknamed "Toffee," who was only eleven months older than me and practically my twin. We used to play together with not-so-fancy toys as one would imagine these days, and listen to mom's bedtime stories. We would then make up our own stories and discuss them with each other. He started writing poetry and publishing handwritten magazines every month, which would circulate only in the family. I wish I had saved some of those. Those were the days! One day he left for heaven but left behind his sweet memories which are still as fresh in my mind as the time they occurred. Had he survived, he would have been a great poet and a writer himself.

I would like to thank my wife, Asma, for her unwavering support, and my genius sons, Niall, Kamil and Rayyan, for their intelligent suggestions and help through fruitful dinner-time discussions during the composition of this book.

Sam Naqvi

Table of Contents

It Was a Long Day...

"...even the longest day has its end."

Irish Proverb

but this one didn't have one...

1

It was a chilly evening on December 31, 2020. I drove to Easton beach on the shores of Rhode Island. Far beyond the land and sea, the sun was setting, closing the curtain on the most turbulent year in recent history. Gentle rising tides moved in a calm sea and the evening birds were returning home, bidding their farewells. Questions loomed over what fate would have in store for us in 2021. Hopes and fears played hide and seek, and the flames of uncertainty flickered ever more violently.

2020 had been an unusual year far beyond my imagination, something I never could have envisioned in my lifetime. It was a year when everyone came together to collectively face a suffering that engulfed the entire globe. This time, countries were not pitched against one another but instead found a common ground as they were up against a common enemy. An enemy that no one could see, yet everyone felt the devastation caused by it. Naturally, the onus fell on the healthcare workers as it concerned health and life in general.

I grew up aspiring to be a doctor from a young age as it was considered a profession which could bring you respectability in society and promised substantial financial stability. I toiled hard and acquired higher qualifications in a bid to achieve excellence in my chosen profession. Life looked good and I was getting on with my profession, and I loved it. Then something unusual and unheard of happened and I found myself at a crossroads for the first time in my life and in my profession.

I had of course read and heard about the Spanish flu causing devastation in the United States, the Black Plague destroying half of Europe. They were fascinating and terrifying stories in history books that were passed down from generation to generation.

Enter Coronavirus and enter the dragon. The time did not seem to fly by this time, and as we lurked in the dark searching for clues and answers, the virus continued to dance on the drums of death.

Authorities worldwide were calling for social distancing, but as a doctor I must nurse the sick. Not only save their lives, but protect myself. Sparse supplies of personal protective equipment (PPE) and lack of prior knowledge of this disease served as roadblocks as the medical community raced against time to save humanity from disaster.

The battle began and went on relentlessly. Fallen heroes were honored while the survivors kept on putting up a fight. 2020 came to an end and still there was no light at the end of the tunnel. Yes, I lived, and lived to tell the tale. The tale of an amazing battle where I must fight against an unseen enemy not just for myself, but for everyone else. Yes, I was there, right there, and I promised myself if I survived, I would one day bring my story to you, the story of "Ground Zero."

Clash of the Titans

When history's greatest superpower finds itself clueless against an unseen tiny enemy, it must lock horns or else face extinction...

2

— • —

On March 10, 2020, routine activities were interrupted in the White House, and it was announced that the President of the United States would address the nation, an event that signaled something really serious was about to happen. The president canceled his private dinner with his vice president and rushed to the oval office. An extraordinary ten-minute speech stunned everyone around the world and sent a shiver down the spine of the bewildered masses. Life took a huge turn.

The address was officially titled: "On the coronavirus Pandemic," and it amounted to the declaration of war against a tiny microbe which was unseen and unknown to the public up until then. Stories had been leaked from China about how a mysterious viral illness had gripped Wuhan, the capital of Hubei province. Suddenly, the public realized it wasn't just some news, it was a real danger.

The ten-minute speech given by the president of the United States highlighted the travel ban from Europe (except the UK) for thirty days. He also announced the extension of health insurance coverage to include treatment for COVID and the waiving of all co-pays for COVID-19, as well as tax relief efforts for small businesses. This was something unusual that had not been witnessed in recent history.

As more events unfolded, it became increasingly obvious that this wasn't going to be just another new viral illness that would be featured in the media now and then and eventually get buried in the leaves of history. The coronavirus exhibited an extraordinary ability to disseminate throughout the community. The speed with which it killed astonished even the most renowned scientists and clinicians in the medical field.

A series of other events and constant news of it on the world stage further endorsed the seriousness of this disease.

Dr. Anthony Fauci of the National Institute of Health, while testifying before congress stated, "The coronavirus outbreak in the US will get significantly worse, and the numbers could be going up and be involved in many millions."

The WHO announced COVID-19 was officially a pandemic.

The Dow Jones Stock market, which had dropped more than 200 hundred points on Monday (March 9, 2020) plunged further down by 2997 points (nearly 13%) on March 16, 2020.

The National Basketball Association game in Oklahoma City between Oklahoma City Thunder and Utah Jazz was canceled before tip-off because of Utah player Rudy Gobert testing positive for the new disease.

These events highlighted the real danger facing United States. The president's speech was a public acknowledgement that United States, the most invincible power on earth ,was under attack, and a declaration of war against the corona virus. In reality it was a pandemic and not just a domestic problem.

As time went on, it became increasingly clear that medical specialists were clueless about this new disease. No prior knowledge existed as to how to prevent or treat this specific disease. Memories of Spanish flu surfaced, and comparisons were quickly drawn, as social distancing along with mask wearing were found to be the only effective way of preventing the spread.

When the president's speech ended, there was complete silence as people were in disbelief, and I heard someone whisper:

"Corona rules the world!"

The battle had begun somewhere else, but now the enemy was at our door, or rather, already among us. War seemed inevitable and uncertainty prevailed. The saga began to unfold.

Rise and Rise of the King

But the conspiracy theorists continue to add fuel to the fire..

3

The appearance of the corona virus on the world stage was very sudden, dramatic, and explosive. Its mysterious appearance and surge raised many eyebrows. Theories upon theories started to pour in. Where was it before? Why has it made a sudden appearance now? What triggered its explosive entry?

Has it been around forever and just turned into a deadly pathogen? Forests of questions kept growing.

Conspiracy theorists were jumping to any conclusions that best suited their fancy for argument. A tale had to be told.

Before we trace the origin of the viral disease let me explain why I prefer to call the virus "King."

In old times there was a famous saying, "Kings have a divine right to rule." What it means is that they were meant to rule due to their birthright bestowed upon them by the God, and no one could take it away from them. Corona is named as such because under microscope the virus displays spike projections around it, which give it the appearance of a crown. Viral armies knew no boundaries and kept marching like a victorious warrior. I do not call it a King out of love for it, but more so as a recognition of its immortality and immense power to disseminate and control the entire globe.

Turning back to the original question, where it came from in the first place, let us turn over the pages in history and try and trace it back to the earliest reports. One would imagine that COVID-19 was only a few months old at the time of outbreak and that all of its history was recorded by websites, accessible through high-speed search engines and modern technology. After all, we are living in an era of computers and high-quality technology. So, one assumes that it must be simple and easy to get to the bottom of the mystery of its origin. Unfortunately, it wasn't, and it was nowhere near that simple.

On December 30th of 2019, Dr. Li Wenliang posted an article in WeChat (an online chat group) to warn that he had seen a report showing positive test results of SARS for seven patients in Wuhan—the capital of Hubei Province in China with a population of eleven million. He was reprimanded by Chinese authorities initially for disrupting public order. Retrospective investigations identified human cases as early as November 2019. On social media it is claimed that the virus originated from the Wuhan Institute of Virology (WIV). Central to the theory is the observation that WIV was in the same city where the earliest known outbreak of the pandemic was recorded. There were reports of coronavirus collected from bats by the scientists for experimentation. There were also claims that some work was being performed on the genome of the virus. How it spread to humans was a mystery. Zoonosis is the term used when a disease is transferred from animals to humans. Well-known examples include: zoonotic influenza, salmonellosis, West Nile virus, bubonic plague, rabies, brucellosis, and Lyme disease. The number of these diseases continues to grow.

Was it an accidental leak or a natural transmission? The conspiracy theorists believe it was a biologic warfare weapon which was developed in secrecy; that it went out of control and backfired. No independent confirmation could be made, as is always the case. Even if it were true, why would anybody confess to it in the first place? After all, it was supposed to be a secret weapon to be unleashed in the event of a significant conflict. Tight-lipped officials remained silent and will probably remain so forever. Internal investigation and reports by the WHO stated this theory is "unlikely." A United States Intelligence Community (IC) probe in October 2021 observed that the Chinese government did not have knowledge of outbreak and the virus likely was not engineered.

Still, some went even further to extrapolate the observation to known history and the entire universe. Were dinosaurs wiped out by a Corona virus pandemic sixty-five million years ago, bringing the cretaceous period to an end after ruling the earth for 245 million years? If so, then where was the virus all this time since then? Are we observing an accurately timed periodic appearance and disappearance of the virus? Did a comet passing by the solar system throw a shower of viruses upon us? Are aliens stationed far away on a distant super "earth" doing experiments on us?

Well obviously, there can't be any independent confirmation of any of these ideas at this time.

So where did it come from? To be honest, at this point in time we don't know. We probably will never know, but the fact of the matter is that corona is real, and it wasn't here before it appeared towards the end of 2019.

Irrespective of its origin, we had to move on, tackle it, tame it, and save the world from its devastation. The enemy this time was deadly, killing quickly with the ability to spread across continents with relative ease, it knew no geographic boundaries. We realized we were up against a clever enemy and a serious threat. It was serious enough to potentially lead humankind to extinction.

DEATH SMILES

"Death smiles at us all, all a man can do is smile back!"

Marcus Aurelius Antoninus Augustus

(Roman Emperor 161 AD-180 AD)

Gladiator, 2000.

4

It was a cold morning on March 12, 2020. News of the corona pandemic had just been acknowledged by the government and all TV channels were pouring out minute-by-minute frenzied coverage of the death toll. The Center for Disease Control (CDC) and healthcare officials were making hurried appearances on TV and social media to advise the public on precautionary measures that they must take. It was a new disease in humans, and no known treatment existed at that time. I hardly saw any vehicles on the road on my way to the hospital. As I parked my car in the parking lot along with a few others, I recognized some of them who were my co-workers in the same hospital. There were hardly any other people in the car park or on the nearby road. They seemed to be in a hurry and wouldn't stop to greet others like they usually would, they only gave a nod of their head and a wave of the hand before they rushed to get away from me. It took me a few good minutes to realize that they were trying to avoid close contact. I finally put into perspective that they were in fact trying to keep their distance. Subconsciously, I was doing the same. It made sense that in the absence of an effective treatment for a new infection your only protection would be to avoid having it transmitted to you. Over the previous few weeks, the media had taken great pains to advocate social distancing and hand washing following every encounter with others. Infections, by definition, are transmissible through contact. A hundred years ago the Spanish flu of 1918 could only be controlled through the implementation of social distancing. Viruses are tough, and compared to bacteria, there are not many effective medications available to combat them. Vaccination and social distancing have remained the mainstay of treatment for about a century. It had become abundantly clear in a relatively brief time that COVID mainly targeted the respiratory system and was transmitted through droplets. In addition to hand washing, it had to be avoided in another effective way. So, it followed that masks were needed for everyone. The question then came up: what type of mask would be more effective? Normal surgical masks were proved inadequate as feedback from China poured in. N95 masks appeared much more effective and were needed in high numbers. Previously they were used by people working in dusty environments and were readily available in shops, but the supply rapidly disappeared from the market as the news of pandemic spread.

In my deep thoughts, I said to myself, *I am a doctor and work for a well-equipped hospital facility, so I shouldn't have to worry about anything.* I entered the hospital through the main entrance and was surprised to find that no one was wearing a mask. At reception I was only greeted with grim smiles and short answers. There was a clear tension in the air. I headed to the corridor on my way to my office. I didn't see many people walking around. In the office, one of my colleague doctors was seated. He only nodded his head in response to my hello. He had a surgical mask on. I had a surgical mask on my desk from before, which I put on as I turned the computer on to get my list of patients. We were hardly talking to each other and when we did, it was only in short sentences. The warmth and closeness that existed before had suddenly evaporated.

We put our white coats on and went out of the room separately on our way to the medical floors for routine rounding. As I walked onto the floor, I heard a female voice ask me, "Where did you get the mask from?"

I turned and saw the nursing manager standing at the other end of the floor. She herself did not have a mask on.

I said, "I had one because I saw a patient a few days back who had the flu."

She said, "We are not supposed to be using any masks."

"What?" I heard my colleague doctor's perplexed voice as he entered onto the floor.

"How do you expect us to see the patients without a mask?" he enquired.

She replied, "The hospital is short on masks and there are clear instructions from management that no healthcare workers should be using a mask."

We were taken aback by this answer. The next few minutes some arguments were exchanged but she insisted there was nothing she could do about it. At the end she remarked that since I had already used the mask I could keep it, but do not take any more. My colleague and I stared at each other in disbelief.

"So basically, we have to see the COVID patients without personal protective equipment?" asked my colleague.

"We don't have enough supplies, unfortunately, so that's how it is."

She shrugged her shoulders and walked away.

This set the tone for the day. On a typical day we see between sixteen to twenty patients each during rounds. This time, every patient looked to be either suffering from COVID or harboring it. The doctors themselves looked scared. To listen to the lungs through a stethoscope the doctor must get close to the patient. It felt like a death warrant had been issued and it would only be a matter of time, probably a short one, until the infection would get to us. As physicians, we cannot hasten through an examination, and the more time you spend close to a potentially infected patient, the more likely you are to contract the infection.

We were left with no choice. Suffering humanity looks to the healthcare workers, particularly doctors—healers. We realized we must fight a new disease without much protection for ourselves.

Walking from floor to floor was not that easy. Thousands of worries were boiling over in our minds.

We must handle the doors aseptically. Infected secretions on contaminated hands could have touched them before us. We carried wipes with us to clean handles, and obviously we were not dealing with just one door and one handle.

Antiseptic hand wash dispensers were running out quickly. The environmental staff was short, so there were clear instructions to use the bare minimum, as necessary.

Families of the patients were banned from the hospital to minimize the risk of transmission, but the COVID patients were succumbing to death quickly. Families were devastated as they could not be by the bedside or even see them one last time before they passed away.

Because of the respiratory nature of the infection and risk of rapid transmission, negative pressure rooms were required, but there weren't many available as no one knew that corona would overwhelm the healthcare resources so rapidly.

Nebulizers couldn't be used as they were believed to hasten the spread of virus. We had to rely on inhalers. Oxygen machines were not in supply to meet the extraordinary demand. ICU ventilators were quickly taken up. It was estimated that anyone who made it to a ventilator would only have a twenty percent chance of survival.

Hospitals were running out of supplies in a fairly short time, and management was finding it hard to keep up with supplies.

As we stared into the eyes of death, there was little hope of a breakthrough. The reports of healthcare workers dying of the disease which they themselves were helping to treat, were increasing. Where would we go from here? Who would succumb first? The patient or the healthcare worker? It was a terrifying question!

Joy of the King

...as mankind struggled to cope with the astonishingly unique challenge, the merciless armies of King corona marched on relentlessly.

5

When I was a little kid, my mom Nargis used to read me bedtime stories. I still remember some of them and may one day share some with you all. My mom's narration was much better than mine and she could easily transport me to the era where that story took place. She used to tell me that one day I could be a writer, but I never believed that. One thing that consistently came up in those stories was that most of them started like this: "Once upon a time, there lived a King who ruled his people ruthlessly." Now, here is the catch for me; I always wondered and asked myself why all these kings were ruthless? Why couldn't they be kind to their own people? I asked this question of my mom one night as she tucked me into the bed and gave me a goodnight kiss. She was about to leave but stopped and turned around. She would not say anything for a few good moments. Rain was pouring heavily that night as the heavens opened. In the dim night light, I could see her face faintly. She appeared to be thinking hard to come up with an answer. Roaring winds outside and the flash of thundering clouds would light up her face from moment to moment. Suddenly a smile broke on her face, and she said that kings behave this way so they can rule through fear. It wasn't until I read *The Prince* by Niccolò Machiavelli that I realized how true that statement was.

How about the King that took the world by storm in 2020? As expected, this King wasn't kind either. After wreaking havoc in China, it turned its reign of terror to other lands and unleashed its ruthless armies across the stormy Atlantic Ocean to land on the shores of the formidable but clueless Superpower. Like Alexander the Great, it loved conquering new lands and locking horns with the most formidable powers on the globe, and it did so indiscriminately. Its hunger, lust for power, and joy of conquering knew no boundaries. No one seemed capable of stopping its march. The death toll continued to rise with every hour. Fun and party-loving, lively Americans underestimated the firepower of the brutal King and virtually ignored the boring lectures on social distancing. Let the American dream live on and spend today as if there is no tomorrow. And why not? Who has seen tomorrow?

COVID spread from state to state, and nothing seemed to work. From east to west coast, the corona spread like a wildfire. The media was finding it hard to cope with the data regarding the death toll and red flag warnings rapidly switched from state to state.

New York became the epicenter of the COVID-19 outbreak in 2020. The first case was reported on February 29, 2020. Between March and May 2020, laboratory confirmed cases reported stood at 203,000 but the actual number was probably much higher than this. The lockdown was imposed from March to April 2020, followed by a four phase re-opening plan by region from April 2020 to July 2020. In October "Micro Cluster Strategy" was implemented, which shut down areas of the state to varying degrees by zip code.

Hospitals were stretched beyond capacity and capability. Morale was running low among Nursing staff who were torn between prioritizing patient care and ensuring the safety of their families and themselves. There weren't enough burial sites. The elderly patients and those with comorbidities succumbed to the virus more easily. The death toll was rising in nursing homes. There were not enough ventilators to meet the demand of the overwhelmed ICUs.

States started to impose inter-state travel bans. Only lockdown, social distancing, PPE, hand washing, and use of ventilators seem to limit the disease. The death toll among healthcare workers continued to mount. Field hospitals were set up.

After July 2020 the other States started to surpass New York. First it was California and later it was Florida and Texas. By the end of 2020, the official US death toll stood at 350,831 though the CDC reported 385,000. The worldwide death toll was estimated to be about three million.

The king lived up to his promise of ruthlessness. Gloom prevailed worldwide as stories poured in from Italy. People turned to God seeking mercy by gathering to sing Hymns. There was despair everywhere and humanity was waiting for a miracle to happen as the best brains still searched for answers which remained evasive.

MAZE RUNNER

...If you are trapped in a giant labyrinth, you have no choice but to run randomly into whichever channel comes first and hope for a light at the end of the tunnel.

...Speed is the essence, but the end is uncertain.

6

Have you ever played in a maze? A maze is a labyrinth and a puzzle of interconnecting paths with a clear entrance and an exit. The challenger is required to come through the entrance and find their way through the branching paths to simpler non-branching patterns that lead to a convoluted layout and eventually, an exit. It can be a fun game for kids or even adults, or a competition for substantial rewards. To play in a maze you don't have to be a genius or a top mathematician like Leonhard Euler. He used his first scientific analysis of a plane maze to lay the foundation of Topology (The study of properties of a geometric object that are preserved under continuous deformations). Mazes are all about enjoyment.

But have you ever been In a maze that you didn't enter by choice, where you had to find your way out? For example, you lost your way, and you came across multiple roads intertwined and crossing each other without any clue as to which one to choose to get home or to the office in time. If you haven't, then I can tell you it's no fun at all. The fun and excitement disappear, and frustration starts to overwhelm you.

How about a situation where you enter a maze against your own will, and you must escape the quandary in a short amount of time, and failure to do so results in your death. The only chance of survival is through finding the exit. It's definitely no fun at all, and that's exactly what I had to face during the pandemic. In this case, it was a question of survival.

As we all know, corona made a sudden and dramatic appearance on the world stage with no one having any prior knowledge of the virus. No known treatment existed. It started in China and quickly spread to the rest of the world at an alarming speed. True, we live in a technically much smaller world which is interconnected through the use of planes, ships, roads, and trains. Distance and travel today are a small endeavor. Of course, that played a big role, but it's the naturally highly transmittable aspect of the virus that made it deadly. There was hardly any time to research and study it properly.

Enter such a maze inadvertently, and the maze will rule you. Every step of the way, multiple paths appeared, but we had no clue which one was right. Without any available treatment, we tried to stick to the basic principles of medicine, which is to preserve life while protecting yourself. It wasn't as easy as it sounds. As we moved from one hurdle to another, we found multiple options and channels, each with a different management plan with hardly any clue as to which option to choose. The medical profession relies on the best available evidence and that comes through studies. In the absence of such studies, one would rely on gut feeling, and this gut feeling is a bit more scientific than that which comes from the non-medical public, because the gut feeling of a healthcare professional is based on prior knowledge of similar situations. This is otherwise called a "best educated guess." That is exactly what we used, though it is not always optimal. Different paths were taken and most of them proved to be just a waste of time, but some of them eventually helped in making progress. The stakes were high, and death was looming. Some hasty studies provided some insights into the disease process, but most of them proved to be wrong overall. As we were meandering in the dark looking for clues, we were met with an imbroglio. The only pandemic guidance we had at that time was from memoirs of the Spanish flu. No doubt social distancing, frequent hand washing, face masks, and the use of antiseptics appeared to be somewhat effective, but they didn't seem to limit the death toll which kept rising. Emerging solutions still did not address the treatment of the active cases. The path that would lead to effective treatment wasn't clear.

One path lead into another and opened into intertwined channels, which seemed to go on forever. There were tunnels after tunnels, but no speck of light. We had to honor and leave the fallen heroes behind. There was no time to look back and the singular question on everyone's mind was, "Is there a light waiting for us at the end of the tunnel?" It was a very good question!

Visibility was Hardly a few Yards

...It was darkness above, below, and all around and not even a faint star to light the path!

7

As corona spread from town to town, from country to country and from continent to continent, the striking thing was that it showed no preference to race, color, religion, age, or sex. Its devastation knew no boundaries. No observational studies could be done in time, as it had appeared quickly.

Though it wasn't the first time that humanity witnessed and suffered from such a devastating infection, breakthroughs in treatment remained elusive for an awfully long time. Comparisons with the Spanish Flu of 1918 were quickly drawn. Lots of research poured into the Flu pandemic at that time, but the Spanish flu continued to rage until April 1920, and four peaks were recorded. The only effective way of containing the flu was through social distancing, quarantine, lock down, isolation, face masks, and judicious use of disinfectants. While all of these practices were quickly implemented this time with coronavirus, variable success was easily interrupted by giant lapses in careful procedure. But, in the absence of an anti-viral drug that could kill the virus, it appeared that a dark fate continued to await us for some time.

As it usually happens, some claims of anti-corona medications surfaced, such as the use of anti-malarial drugs, vitamin D, Zinc, and Ivermectin—but all quickly proved to be futile. In fact, the observation that some deadly complications happened from the use of these medications led to general despair among the medical community and the public. Little hope was found.

There was news of various studies being set up, not just in United States, but across the world. None of these results were encouraging or promising.

There is no doubt that scientists, virologists, biologists, and many others were working day and night behind the scenes to discover or rediscover a magic medicine that would kill the virus.

Intense competition had started amongst the pharmaceutical companies to get ahead of each other as it was widely believed that anyone who developed such a medicine first would bring astronomical riches to the company.

The worldwide race was on, but this race took time. While all these efforts were being made behind the scenes, it made hardly any difference to the public and healthcare workers' psyches.

"We want results, not complex talks," was the general public's opinion. Nothing was in sight to look forward to.

Where do we go from here? No one knew the answer.

As mankind drove through the thickest fog, visibility was barely a few yards, so to speak.

THE KING BREATHES FIRE

...When the King's armies marched, the world lay at its feet waiting to be conquered...

...and who would dare stop the galloping shiny chariot the King was riding on?

8

━ • ━

My childhood was like a dream state. My brother Javed and I were about eleven months apart and we were chums. We were very fond of stories and imagination. We used to try and finish our homework quickly and play together with toys until bedtime. After dinner, mom used to tell us stories. They seemed to us like real-life events and would transport us to another world. Some of these stories were about kings and their armies, who would conquer one land after another. They sounded fascinating. Who wouldn't love a victorious king, especially when listening to these stories in the comfort of your home?

As the childhood mist and fog began to clear up and the real essence of wars and the facts, figures, and numbers started to make sense, the castles in the air started tumbling down. For a king to win and conquer, the magnitude of killings that are required is a gruesome fact that is un-matched.

Imagine a situation where you are part of a losing empire about to fall to the devastating armies of a victorious and unstoppable king? It is horrific, and that's where we were in our pandemic.

King's Journey begins in China.

It all started somewhere in December 2019 when a previously unknown mysterious viral illness was reported by Chinese authorities. The legend says it started in the Hunan seafood wholesale market in Wuhan, though no roots could be traced. China identified a novel Coronavirus on January 7th, 2020, as the cause of illness and temporarily named it 2019-nCOV. Weeks later, January 30, 2020, the World Health Organization (WHO) declared it a public health emergency of international concern. No one could imagine at that time that it would grow to such monstrous proportions.

On February 11, 2020, corona got its first official name, SARS-CoV2 (severe acute respiratory syndrome) and the disease was named COVID-19 (to signify the year when it started).

To most people, it still looked like one of those serious infections which will eventually contain itself, die down, and may not even qualify to be mentioned seriously in history books. But that wasn't the case.

Corona invades Europe.

On February 4, 2020, the cruise ship "Diamond Princess" was made to anchor off the coast of Yokohama by Japanese authorities. 712 people out of the 3,711 aboard tested positive. A quarantine was ordered.

On February 25, 2020, H10 Costa Adeje Palace hotel on the Island of Tenerife, with 1,000 guests and workers at the hotel, was put on lockdown after an Italian doctor and his wife tested positive.

The world had already become aware of the mysterious illness in China, but these instances alarmed the international community.

The genie had already been let out of the bottle.

By late February of 2020, the pandemic exploded in Italy and eight other European countries including Belgium, Finland, France, Germany, Russia, Spain, Sweden, and the UK. Each of these countries reported alarmingly increasing numbers of cases daily.

In Italy, Province of Lombardy, a regional Lockdown was enforced on March 8th, and many countries closed off their borders to Italy.

The World Health Organization (WHO) declared Europe as the Epicenter of the Pandemic on March 11, 2020, and the US imposed a travel ban from the Schengen area.

Italy took the worst hit. The alarming nature of the situation was highlighted when doctors said they had to pick and choose who to treat due to rapidly overflowing hospitals. A fifty-seven year old Italian doctor, Marcello Natali, told the press that he was forced to work without gloves due to lack of supplies. He eventually died in Codogno.

Belgium closed schools, Spain declared emergency and shut restaurants and schools, German Chancellor Angela Markel named COVID-19 as the biggest challenge, the UK announced lockdown. Hungarian Prime Minister Viktor Orbán passed a law to give himself sweeping powers to control the pandemic.

Europe will never forget March 2020, when life changed so much. By April, half of humanity was under lockdown and hundreds of deaths were being reported daily. By mid-April global cases exceeded two million and the death toll exceeded 100,000.

USA welcomes the victorious King.

By March 2020, China reported a significant drop in the number of cases, but the battle ground had already moved to Europe and the USA. On February 29, 2020, the CDC confirmed the first person to die of COVID in Washington State. By March, New York had become the Epicenter. A national lockdown was imposed in March 2020. Hospitals were running out of supplies. Depression was gripping our healthcare workers. Field hospitals were set up. Thousands of new cases and hundreds of deaths were reported each day. The elderly were hit the hardest. Between March and May of 2020, about 203,000 Lab confirmed cases were reported to the NYC Department of Health & Mental Hygiene.

It took no time for the virus to spread to the other states and by July, California, Florida, and Texas were the worst hit. The official death toll, per the CDC, stood at 350, 831, but was estimated to really be around 385,000. The worldwide death toll was reported to be 1,813,188 but estimates suggest the actual number was at least three million (1.2 million more than officially reported).

King marches into South America

In late May 2020, COVID exploded in Rio de Janeiro and Sao Paulo. 300,000 cases and 19,000 deaths were reported in Brazil in May 2020. Brazil was declared the epicenter of pandemic. The most affected areas were the Sao Paulo region, States of Rio de Janeiro, Cearra, Amazonas, and Pernambuco.

Venezuela, Columbia, Ecuador, Peru, Bolivia, Chile, and Argentina all reported significantly high case numbers and deaths.

Overall, Brazil eventually had 12.8 million confirmed cases with more than 325,000 deaths, second only to the USA.

Continent of Africa

The very first COVID-19 case was recorded on February 14, 2020, in Egypt, followed by first confirmed case in Sub-Saharan Africa was announced in Nigeria at the end of February 2020. Within 3 months the virus had spread throughout the continent, as Lesotho, the last African sovereign State to have remained free of the virus, reported a case on May 13, 2020. The countries that were hit hardest were South Africa, Egypt, Morocco, Ethiopia, Nigeria, and together these 5 countries accounted for 75% of confirmed cases. More than one million confirmed cases were reported across the continent by August 6, 2020. WHO voiced alarm at the spread in Africa on July 20, 2020, stating South Africa's surging numbers could be precursor for further outbreaks across the continent. Africa houses seventeen percent of the global population but reported five percent of global cases and three percent of global deaths.

A relatively lower number was attributed to African governments that took early public health measures to prevent the transmission. Additionally, most African countries routinely manage infectious disease outbreaks and have expertise in isolation, quarantine and contact tracing.

India

The lockdown was announced in Kerala in March 2020. By late April, India led the world in new cases. In April 2020, India had more than 2.5 million cases.

Russia

At the end of March 2020, a lockdown was imposed in Russia. By April the number of cases exceeded three million.

I deliberately left out Australia and New Zealand as there is an entirely different story to tell later in this book.

King corona originated mysteriously somehow in Wuhan and spread like a jungle fire across the world, and nothing seemed to stop its march. As the King was breathing fire, mankind appeared clueless, and it seemed that only a miracle could save the world.

Oasis in the Raging Fires

...when the rampant king's armies roamed the earth, it wasn't all lost in a remote corner.

9

Those early days were tough and hard days. The world was in turmoil and King Corona continued to advance relentlessly. I could see stress on everyone's face. There was news of intense research into COVID behind the scenes, but no results were coming forth and it was only adding to the frustration of the public.

When these raging fires engulfed the entire globe, some pockets of resistance appeared like an oasis in the burning desert. It appeared too good to be true.

While the continent of Africa remained less affected than others, Australia and in particular, New Zealand, sprung some surprises. At one point, I asked one of my colleagues why New Zealand was not as badly affected while we are suffering so much here in USA. His reply made sense, "They have a smart girl who nailed it down." He was referring to the New Zealand Prime Minister. Someone jokingly said, "Lets hire her for a per diem shift here in the USA."

The first case of COVID appeared in New Zealand on February 28, 2020, and the government immediately closed borders and imposed a two-month nationwide lockdown. Regionalized alert level changes were introduced from March 16th to March 19th.

New Zealand eliminated COVID in week twenty-four of the pandemic (June 2020). This was a time when the rest of the world was severely affected by corona; this was a watershed moment.

How did they achieve these results? Well, this can be attributed to many factors.

New Zealand is a relatively geographically isolated country, and they took early measures including stringent public health interventions, early border closure, nationwide lockdown, prompt isolation of cases, and tracing of contacts. Technically this may not have been possible for a country like the USA or the European States, where countries are virtually merged into each other.

It's next-door giant neighbor, Australia, was not too far behind. Biosecurity officials began screening passengers coming from China, especially Wuhan to Sydney. Australia saw two distinct peaks from March-April and from June-October in 2020, but the disease burden and mortality rates remained low. A total of 28,500 cases and 900 deaths appeared modest when compared to other countries. The same reasons, as was the case with New Zealand, have been deemed responsible for the much more successful outcome and management of the disease than what was seen in the rest of the world.

Maybe it instilled a little hope in us at that time that King corona may not be as invincible as we thought.

It's true that the disease burden remained low in some regions (and was possibly due to smart thinking), but corona did invade those areas and we still didn't have a killer cure.

We were desperately looking for answers and each corner we turned appeared to lead to another one. We kept asking, where is the end? Is there one at all?

"Is a Sagittarian like me going to give up?" I would ask myself, though I hardly ever believed in Astrology. Optimism is a trait of Sagittarians, and supposedly, ruling Jupiter could one day bring abundance and luck to me. I am not sure whether that is true or not, but one thing I have is perseverance. Even in the face of adversity, I look for a silver lining in thunderous dark clouds, and I did it this time as well. This was a time when people started to ask me, "Are we heading towards extinction?" Or, "Is it an 'extinction level' event?"

EXTINCTION LEVEL EVENT

...will the world finally come to an end?

...are we paying a price for our sins as Noah's sons did?

10

▬ ● ▬

….a long time ago there lived a civilization that was so advanced that they could fly through the air, build giant buildings, bridges, and canals, travel the oceans with clear precision and speed, and carve out statues from mountains, but then all of a sudden, this civilization ended abruptly. Layers upon layers and traces of their remains show up but then there is absolutely nothing in the penultimate layer. What happened to them? How did they become extinct suddenly? What was it that caused their sudden disappearance from the face of the earth? No evidence of the giant building's destruction or natural catastrophe could be found. So, what caused the dramatic exit of such a clever civilization which roamed and dominated the earth for a long period of time? It's puzzling,

*and a great unsolved mystery of gigantic propor-
tions as they did not leave any clue behind which
could shed light on their extinction...*

Archaeologists of the future would be scratch-
ing their heads and asking millions of related
questions if they were to dig up the remains of our
era should it have come to an end by this, one of
the deadliest pandemics.

Nature has an awesome power as we have
seen in history. Malthusian theory of population
offers a clue, though serious doubts have been
cast on it. Thomas Malthus was an English philosopher in the eighteenth to nineteenth century. He
linked exponential growth of the population to
arithmetic food supply growth. He argued that
positive checks on human population like epidem-
ics, famines, wars, earthquakes, floods, and natural calamities do not allow the population to over-
grow whenever the food supply drops below critical levels. He also talked about preventative
checks which humans can employ such as late
marriages, simple living, and self-control to avoid
the natural forces putting clamps on population
growth through destructive events. Obviously,
there were serious questions about the validity of
this theory, but there is some element of truth to

it. Was the corona virus pandemic of 2020 a natural check like the one Thomas Malthus spoke of?

Known human history is studded with catastrophes and natural and man-made disasters. In the late eighteenth century, Baron Georges Cuvier, French naturalist and biologist, in his essay on *The Theory of the Earth* (1813) proposed that since creation, the earth has encountered repeated mass extinctions brought on by periodic natural disasters. He is considered by many to be the founding father of Paleontology. Convincing evidence suggests that countless animals existed in the past but then disappeared from the face of the earth.

The biggest puzzle of all time that came to everyone's mind was the sudden disappearance of the dinosaurs. It's a kid's dream to talk about dinosaurs, but adults are not very far behind in this discussion. The dinosaurs who are believed to have evolved from reptiles sometime in the Triassic period, which ended about 200 million years ago, would roam the earth in next era—the Jurassic period. They were the most versatile animals and undisputed rulers of the earth. For the next seventy million years, they demonstrated the ability to produce wave after wave of new species until the end of the Cretaceous period when they suddenly disappeared. For a puzzled mind the question kept arising; what was it that caused their sudden exit? This is a serious question because if a periodic extinction indeed occurs on a regular basis, then it can happen to humans as well.

Natural disasters are the most plausible potential causes of extinction. Could it have been a meteorite that hit earth and raised a dust storm, blocking sunlight for years leading to a worldwide food shortage, or did they develop some connective tissue disorder through mutation and start producing fragile and non-viable eggs? Or was it a pandemic of infection that wiped them out? Could it have been the corona virus or a similar virus that led to their extinction? Is the same demon rearing its head yet again?

There is a lot more to say about disasters that shook the earth. One could be drawn to events like the drying and vanishing of the Mediterranean Sea basin, the plague of Athens and London, the earthquake of Alexandria, the black death, the influenza pandemic, the Krakatoa volcanic eruption, famine in China, and the tsunami terror in Japan, to name a few.

Some science theories state that one single piece of land existed on earth about 200-300 million years ago when Europe, Asia, Africa, and South and North America were merged into one single continent which split due to tectonic plate movement, causing the continents to drift apart. No humans were believed to have existed at that time. The event highlights the cataclysmic power of nature and the very fact that it could happen again, which puts a question mark on our own survival.

There is evidence in archeology that many civilizations reached a peak and then some natural disaster or internal conflicts brought them to an end. Who can deny the ability of ancient Egyptians to build giant pyramids with such pinpoint accuracy and to preserve their dead ones' bodies to last more than a millennium. Where did all that knowledge go? The ruins tell the magnificence of lost civilizations. The buildings, tools, statues, monolithic gigantic rocks, arrangement of structures with astronomical significance, use of numbers, wall paintings, and writings tell us that they had an extraordinary knowledge of science. What happened to them then? Why did they vanish?

The biggest question is, can it happen to us as well?

People seriously believed at the height of the pandemic that COVID had the potential to grow to cataclysmic proportions and wipe out humans.

There is evidence in medicine that viruses and bacteria worldwide come in waves, span for a significant length of time, and go away. Discovery of the first antibiotic Penicillin in 1928 didn't eradicate bacterial infections from the face of earth, though it was claimed by a congressman of that time.

You can let your mind wander and imagine a number of scenarios, however, if you are in a real-time life-threatening situation, then it's all different. People seriously started asking, "Will the world come to an end? Will mankind survive in its current form to transmit information about this pandemic to the next generation?" How would humans fight back if there were no signs that the virus could be controlled? If human history's greatest superpower cannot tame corona, then who would do it instead? Is the superpower so hapless?

HAPLESS SUPERPOWER

"...we have plenty of food, so why are grocery store shelves so empty?"

MarketWatch

11

The adaptability and proactiveness of a person, a town, a nation, a league of nations, or even the entire world, can be discovered if they are subjected to an extreme emergency like a credit crunch, sudden war, a pandemic, or a natural disaster. Corona exposed many nations in their lack of preparation and caution in regards to public health emergencies. Not surprisingly, these included some of the most highly developed countries. The USA was no exception.

A nation with a fleet of naval ships, state-of-the-art fighter jets, ultra-sophisticated armory, highly trained armies, and satellite links of high precision, appeared completely hapless and dumbfounded. Our previous experience and expertise on infectious diseases seemed to have been forgotten, buried under the dust of history to have little effect, if any, on the preparedness for another pandemic.

Empty shelves in grocery stores and retail markets told the story of the inability to keep peace with the turn of events. Panic buying essential goods in bulk forced businesses to limit customers' purchases. Toilet paper, milk, and bread disappeared from the market. On some level, it was as if war time rationing was in place, and purchasers saw a steep rise in their prices.

Businesses started to shut down as the workforce fell ill. Cash starved small businesses were unable to meet demands and invest in the market as prices continued to rise.

Disinfectants disappeared from the shelves and gas prices soared.

PPE was in severe shortage, even in hospitals and healthcare facilities. Healthcare workers (HCW) were asked not to use PPE until supplies increased. Amnesty International published a report on July 13, 2020, showing more than 3,000 HCW deaths worldwide, raising safety concerns for everyone. The countries that ranked in the top three were Russia (545), UK (540) and USA (507) in HCW deaths.

No medications were available that could effectively treat coronavirus. The medication falsely reported to be effective against corona was chloroquine. It disappeared from the market as soon as the rumors circulated. That is a long story, but its use was met with poor results, and even some deaths. The use of it eventually stopped.

Pharmaceutical companies were tightlipped about vaccine trials and open communication was limited. The details of how trials were carried out were kept in secrecy. This alarmed both scientists and the general public. Safety concerns were raised. Governments stayed relatively quiet and would only release statements when it came to sharing research credit. Pharmaceutical companies were openly denying that governments provided federal funds for vaccine development. Governments and pharmaceutical companies appeared to be in loggerheads.

The reporting of statistics on the COVID pandemic by each government was not entirely clean either, unfortunately. According to some claims, some false statistics were reported to have been produced to conceal deaths in nursing homes and rehab centers.

COVID test kits were in severe shortage and were only allocated to big hospitals and institutions.

There was a clear lag between statements and action. Field hospitals could not be set up by reserve military forces swiftly at a time when the whole country was simmering with COVID victims.

Contrary to all of this, morale among healthcare workers remained high despite the lack of adequate support that was needed at that stage. There were heartbreaking, horrific stories of healthcare workers succumbing to the disease during the execution of their duties without any support from authorities with timely and adequate supplies of PPE.

Without going into politics, the overall management of a catastrophe of this proportion was poor and reflected a clear unpreparedness on the part of most of the governments worldwide.

People on trips to other countries got stranded away from their homes and had no idea when they would see their loved ones. A very well-known example is when actor and film maker

Tom Hanks got stuck in Australia after he and his wife contracted COVID.

Schools were indefinitely closed, and children's education was in jeopardy. Keeping children busy at home was not an easy task for the parents. The conflict between carrying out jobs and looking after children at home became a big issue. Remote learning was introduced but elementary school children transitioning into middle schools were not familiar with the technology and neither were their parents.

Thrown into the mix were claims by the healthcare workers of unfair pay and compensations for their services at a time which was particularly stressful for them.

It was all confusion and chaos. Misinformation abounded, and it was rampant. In a compelling environment like that what would a doctor like me do? Help others, or protect myself and my family? What would you have done if you were in my place? Time stood still, the path was rough and the destination still elusive. The journey through the torrid and turbulent time to come was just beginning.

WHEN TIME STOOD STILL!

...an emotional journey through the turbulent times.

12

Time flies, but it leaves indelible prints. The past always looks like a golden page that we do not want to let go of when we look back on our lives, even when it reminds us of some difficult times. It was a survival game. "The struggle for existence and survival of the fittest" was the order of the day. A "winner takes it all" situation never meant so much as it did during that time. The year 2020 whizzed past me and felt like just one long "night without end."

So, where do I start? There are a million tiny events that could be stitched together, but when you are trying to undo a tangled mass of tiny threads it simply makes it worse.

As we saw earlier, the news of corona had already started to come out of China by the end of 2019 but was not taken seriously in the West initially. News of serious infections like Ebola, for example, had previously made it to the headlines but never raised serious concern as they mainly remained confined to certain geographic locations. As the news of corona spreading to Italy came out, suddenly everyone realized that the Genie was already out of the lamp. It was like a bombshell dropped on our heads.

The healthcare institutions were called into action as there was no one else who could deal with such a situation.

My first day at work, since the public acknowledgement of corona as a serious threat, was a nightmare, as I previously wrote. My life was shifting into an entirely new routine with self-imposed new rules that I must follow to find a balance between personal & family safety, morale, and commitments. This would require a strong work ethic and effort on my part to save our ailing humanity from disaster.

Schools were shut down indefinitely and children got confined to their homes. Distant learning became the main tool for children's education. I had to help my kids with distance learning, which was new for me myself, and at the same time I had to give them enough company to keep their spirits and morale high.

With the kids staying at home, I had to make sure that I had enough food and snacks at home to feed them.

As a doctor, I was inevitably going to be exposed to COVID patients all the time and since it is a transmissible disease, I had to make sure that I didn't contract the disease and at the same time I also had to avoid carrying it with me to the house and transferring it to my children. This was not an easy task, especially when PPE was increasingly difficult to get, and disinfectants were in short supply both in the market and at healthcare institutions.

A steady cash flow is always necessary to keep going in life. The positive side of the disastrous situation, if any, is that it kept me in the job as it was a medical super emergency and I was needed by others, more than any other time in my life. At times I felt heartbroken for people who could not carry out their jobs, or those whose businesses got shut down.

As the days went by, I unknowingly got into a kind of robot-like routine. I would get up in the morning and wake the children up to get them ready for their distant learning school, which was carried out through the computer and internet. I would then get them breakfast and prepare their lunch beforehand and give them instructions. Then I would drive to work. The roads at the time were relatively empty on my way to the hospital. Only the front door of the hospital was allowed as a single-entry point into the building. I somehow got a mask that I would use for several days. I would disinfect my hands at the front door. Everyone was seen trying to keep away from each other. If the mask slipped down, then people would point out from a distance to fix it. I would go to my office, which I shared with other fellow doctors, and print my list of patients. We were trying to keep the conversation to a minimum to avoid transmission of infection. Our masks were on all the time. Some doctors brought their own supplies of disinfectants and PPE and were visibly uneasy at the prospect of sharing with others. In the coffee room only two people were allowed in at any time while others would wait outside for their turn.

After printing the patient list, I would make my way to the medical floor. Touching door handles, banisters at stairs, buttons and side bars at elevators appeared to be an obvious risk. I would carry a disinfectant wipe to clean the door handles before using them. I would not dare to touch the bannisters and bars. No more than two or three people were considered safe in an elevator.

Going from room to room during ward round was becoming more and more of a task as we had to disinfect our hands, keep our masks on, and wear gowns. To examine a patient, you needed to get close to them to listen to their lungs and heart. Corona affected the lungs the most, and that is where the risk lied the heaviest. We had to disinfect the stethoscope and other equipment after seeing each patient. Seeing and rounding on eighteen to twenty patients during every shift in such conditions was no fun.

COVID patients required isolation in negative pressure rooms to minimize risk of transmission. The hospitals were in dire shortage of such rooms. Rounding on active COVID patients was a serious challenge. COVID meant a virtual death warrant at that time. There was risk of transmission of infection through literally anything that you would carry into their rooms. Hair must be covered with disposable hats, N 95 masks must be on, Eye and face shield needed to be worn though their supplies came late to the HCWs for routine use. Every disposable thing must be disposed of and non-disposables must be disinfected before and after clinical encounter.

Medicine is all about preserving life and health and nothing can be more dramatic than an acute emergency arising while doing routine work. It happens all the time during a healthcare worker's shift. The term "Code" is used for emergency situations like that, and colors are assigned to the type of emergency. For example, Code blue means patient is pulseless and not breathing and it requires action within seconds to preserve life. The term BAT is used for Bed Side Assistance when a patient requires emergency assistance but is self-breathing and has a pulse. These calls were becoming common during the COVID pandemic, and little time would be available to HCWs to use protective measures. Emergency intubation for artificial breathing and transfer to Intensive Care was becoming more and more frequent. ICUs were running short of ventilators (artificial breathing machines). Every time HCWs had to respond to such emergencies it was by no means certain to predict how many of them got infected themselves. COVID patients who had to be intubated were considered to have only a twenty percent chance of survival.

The whole day and every moment used to be a war-like situation for us. There were no effective drugs available at that time. We were dealing with an unseen tiny microbe without any clue as to how it caused that disease or how to control and eventually treat it.

The news of healthcare workers succumbing to the disease worldwide was heart breaking and severely dented the confidence and morale of some. A real-life threat existed for every one of us.

The end of each shift didn't bring any reprieve either. We were heading home having been heavily exposed to the infection. Stories of infection being transmitted from surfaces and cell phones were common. We had to disinfect ourselves before entering our vehicles and heading home. I would change my clothes in the parking garage and use disinfectants to decontaminate myself and when I arrived home, I'd make my way to the shower without even talking to anyone or touching anything. A separate shower was used for this purpose.

All of the TV channels were committed to minute-by-minute reporting on the pandemic and sharing the latest information available. Interviews with health authorities, experts of infectious diseases, patients that survived, and those who lost their loved ones, were flowing through the channels like floods. Few clues were coming in as to what would be the best way of dealing with COVID.

Many of our colleagues got infected themselves and had to be quarantined. That would put additional workloads on others as replacing staff wasn't that simple during those times.

I was also working in an outpatient clinic part time. I shared the office with another doctor and one day I saw him coughing and I asked him, *"Are you OK?"* He said he was not feeling well. Instant COVID tests were not available at that time. He went for the test, but the result wouldn't be available for a couple days. He stopped coming in, meanwhile our clinic secretary said she was running low grade fevers and another one of my fellow doctor colleagues also reported having a fever. The doctor in our clinic called me after two days to inform me that he had tested positive. Our secretary tested positive as well, and so did my colleague at the hospital. It was a serious situation as we had to shut down the clinic. We had to resort to telemedicine, which I had to do from home computer. This went on for months. Luckily, insurance companies accepted telemedicine as an alternative and that kept the clinic going from a business standpoint.

My fellow doctor in the hospital who tested positive was not the only one affected, his wife and all his children also tested positive, and he had to confine himself at home along with his entire family.

Stories like this were very common in those days and it felt as if it was only a matter of time before you might get infected yourself. My friends abroad and all over the world were reporting such incidents.

Each day felt long, and by the time the day was over I would be ready for another tough day at work.

COVID tests were carried out at specified centers, and you could only drive through and get tested while sitting in your car, but the results wouldn't be available for two or three days. I had to drive my kids several times for testing and every time life would hang in balance until I got the results. Instant tests were not available at that time and there were talks of home testing kits, but they wouldn't be available for several months.

Life had gone into a monotonous routine with few clues as to where we were heading and when it would end. Time stood still and we were meandering in the dark searching for answers. Where was the destination? It was indeed a very good question at that time.

I wanted to turn back the clocks and have the same lively and vibrant America back with laughter, fun, energy, play rides, the Superbowl, and games under lights. Where were those noisy restaurants with the fragrance of delicious food in the air? The beaches simmering with sun and sand and sunbathing bodies turned into ghastly haunted areas. Where did it all go? Would the American dream rise again and live on?

RISE OF THE MACHINES!!!

"...when one door closes, fortune will usually open an-other."

Alexander Graham Bell quoting Fernando de Rojas in
La Celestina

...when a tiny microbe wreaked havoc, machines came to the rescue of humans.

13

Technology could easily be deemed our best friend and our worst enemy at the same time. Human history has seen a steep rise of machines in parallel with human societal development and more so during times of stress.

Now almost everyone is not only aware of Zoom and Skype conferences but is actively using them as well.

During the COVID-19 pandemic, there was an exponential rise in use of video conferences, interviews, distance learning, and Telemedicine. This was out of necessity. Isolation was the only known effective means to prevent the spread, and Lockdowns led to isolation of professionals and students. As is commonly said "the show must go on" there had to be an alternate way of communication while maintaining safety. Technology bridged the gap during hardest times of the pandemic.

Telemedicine became a very common practice during COVID times, not only in the hospitals but for outpatient care as well. Doctors could visit their patients virtually through video cameras, talk to them, give advice, and plan care management. We had this technology before, but it advanced significantly during COVID times. It gave patients access to care while minimizing the risk of exposure to infection. This gave patients great peace of mind as they could still directly interact with healthcare professionals.

Nobody can deny the importance of kids' education. They are the builders and pillars of tomorrow. Because of COVID, children were forced to stay at home. That's when virtual learning became a necessity rather than a privilege.

Distance learning is not new. Relevant literature research tells us that it began in 1728 with the Boston Gazette sending weekly mailed lessons. Computer technology has led to video conferencing and virtual meetings. Most schools turned to virtual learning during the pandemic. There were significant issues as the children and their parents didn't have full understanding of how it would work. Elementary school children were particularly affected as they transitioned into Middle schools. This was a big jump for them. Parents were getting emails that children did not complete their homework while children were insisting that they had done it. Another issue was that internet was not available to all children and parents for financial reasons.

Technology also helped businesses to carry out interviews and conferences. Interviews for recruiting became virtual almost everywhere, and even now this remains widely practiced. Business conferences and advice from experts were delivered by virtual means more and more.

The use of technology extended to communities, religious services, and family meetings for happy occasions and bereavements alike.

The idea that you could join others for a meeting even when people are miles apart seemed too good to be true. Thanks to technology, we have access that puts us closer together than ever before.

Scientists and specialists could communicate directly, and this made a significant difference in the development of a vaccine. While pharmaceutical companies hate to share their preliminary data with other companies, technology played a huge role in improving communication within the pharmaceutical companies' own circles.

Necessity is the mother of invention, as is commonly said. One invention leads to another one. During COVID times the machines came through for the humans who had invented them. A favor well returned!

The King Hits the Pocket Hard

...if you want to destroy the enemy, destroy its resources.

14

"Now you will understand the value of money!" My dad said to me, smiling, while giving me a fancy piggy bank as a birthday gift. I did not realize that my first lesson of economics had already been delivered to me. His next statement was even more stunning and baffling: _"Understand the value of money but do not indulge in love of money!"_

A further shock awaited me:

"There is no such thing as free lunch!"

My little mind was grappling with these new ideas.

"But I do get free lunch from you, don't I?" Confused as I was, I asked in haste. He replied: _"You will pay it back when you give to your own children."_

Real life economics is much more painful than this. Hard facts do not smile upon you, especially at a time of credit crunch.

I am no expert on economics, but economics will always get you one way or another. If you have a guardian angel, it might not bother you for some time, but if you are the main breadwinner, it does affect you. Money comes hard but disappears fast.

2020 was a particularly difficult time for families, especially for small business owners. The world economy as a whole and the US economy experienced big setbacks and slumps.

The lockdown and social distancing were major tools to prevent spread of the disease and that required the closure of shops and business offices, which led to shortage of workforce. Investments in private businesses started to decline with diminishing returns.

Without going into hardcore details, I will briefly highlight a few facts. There are five economic indicators that provide insight into the situation that unfolded.

1. **GDP** fell by 8.9 % in the second quarter of the year 2020.

2. **Consumption** saw a huge decline of 54% in spending on restaurant dining.
3. **Investments** declined during the early part of the COVID pandemic in 2020. Some figures gathered here from my internet search show a twenty percent decline in office structures, a thirty percent decline in multi-merchandise shopping, and a thirty-three percent decline in spending at food & beverage establishments. Investment in other sectors including mining (oil & gas), religious/educational structures, lodging, industrial & transportation equipment, artistic originals and investment in research and development, also markedly declined.
4. **International Trade** slumped and imports increased while exports dropped, widening the trade deficit.
5. **Stability** saw major setbacks in supply of money, prices, and federal government budgets.

The above facts indicate the negative effects on the world economy, as well as the US economy, during COVID times. The economy did recover afterwards, but price hikes in virtually every commodity that were seen at that time continued to haunt the public, even as I wrote this book. The rise in inflation was significantly higher than the previous year's average.

A little note to acknowledge that though we saw decline in investment of major enterprises, but relatively smaller decline in health structures and industries was noticed as per economic indicators. It makes sense as logically a health hazard can only be offset by more investment in healthcare industry.

As the COVID pandemic progressed, stories of hardships that the families were facing continued to surface in the media. Unfortunately, the situation was far worse in developing countries for obvious reasons.

An economic meltdown leads to chaos, but the will to survive brings people together. This was particularly evident during COVID times. Facing the calamity together was less painful than doing it alone. Economic hardships troubled everyone, and the battle was on, but mutual love grew stronger!

"Back In the Saddle Again!"

I was a cool cowboy riding the range, shepherding my longhorn cattle feeding on lowly gypsum weed, and then it all became dark and gloomy when I was pushed to the corner and I was back in the saddle again to take on the carnage, and my buddies stood like rocks alongside me and fought off the unprecedented assault with bare hands.

Gene Autry

15

— • —

Mankind was locked in an unprecedented, epic battle with an unseen enemy who kept its upper hand. As gigantic armies watched in awe with their fearsome stealth bombers remained grounded, destroyers were docked on the shores or floated aimlessly, and not even a single shot was fired when the ill-equipped healthcare workers moved to the battle front empty handed. They had no armor to protect them, only a brave heart and the will to fight till the end stood between death and victory.

Those were trying times. We were fighting with our backs against the wall. The dramatic appearance of corona posed a major challenge. The unpreparedness of healthcare institutions including hospitals, offices, nursing homes, rehabilitation & transfusion centers and labs was blatantly exposed. The healthcare institutions were finding it hard to keep up with supplies, including therapeutic and protective equipment.

If the bugle of war had already been blown, would you wait for the armory to arrive? The bull had to be taken by the horns, without delay. We had to fight not just for others, but for ourselves as well, and we did. Things look very romantic in a cowboy tale, where an unbeatable horse rider with his sombrero, locked in a titanic rough rodeo while toting a 44-magnum gun, can weather any storm. It is all a much different feeling when you are in it.

My healthcare friends risked their lives to fight a battle that history will never forget. They needed unwavering faith to win the battle. Fallen heroes" losses would not dent the resolve of the warriors. The lack of equipment, shortage of supplies, exhaustion from burn out, psychogenic trauma, stress, time pressure, lack of work-home balance, work overload, and absence of infrastructure, were the barriers that they had to overcome. It became a hurdle race.

As previously mentioned, Amnesty International published a report in July 2020 reporting more than 3,000 healthcare worker's deaths, which was believed to be a gross underestimate of real loss of lives of healthcare workers. A global shortage of PPE was reported along with it. Trade restrictions by some countries had complicated the situation further.

In the words of an Egyptian doctor "Healthcare workers had to choose between death or jail." Reprisals were reported for those who failed to attend shifts, and for speaking out about poor working conditions, posting on social media, or voicing objections. Doctors recounted threats delivered via WhatsApp, official letters, or in person. They were told that such acts would result in complaints to the National security Agency of Egypt. Rights group reported that multiple healthcare workers were arrested.

Health workers, in some situations, faced a stigma and violence was reported in some cases. A Mexican nurse was reported to have been drenched in chlorine while walking down the street. In another incident that was reported, a hospital utility worker was smeared with bleach.

But there were also reports of love and appreciation by the public as well. I was coming off my shift one day, and I had to stop by a shop to get some groceries. My hospital badge was around my neck. A woman saw it and came up to me and said, "Thank you so much for protecting and looking after us. You are our heroes." Others who were gathered around also expressed gratitude and their love melted my heart.

I also remember seeing footage from China where the security personnel lined up and saluted the healthcare workers for their heroic efforts.

I will never forget those acts of commitment, bravery and heroism from health workers who did not even care for their own safety and gave more than one-hundred percent to the ailing population.

Hats off to those brave warriors.

Eureka! Eureka! Eureka!

...as I was lurking in the dark, I stumbled upon a mind-blowing discovery. Could it be the clue?

16

Somewhere during the year 246 BC, a Sicilian from Syracuse (Italy), while sitting in a bath, discovered a clue about a puzzle which he had been pondering for some time. It was so overwhelming that he ran naked out of the bath, shouting, "Eureka! Eureka! Eureka!" to tell the king about his sensational discovery. He was arguably one of the greatest mathematicians of all time, the legendary Archimedes.

In the late summer of 1666, a young farm boy observed an apple fall from its tree to the ground. He wondered, *why did it fall?* A "Eureka moment" for Isaac Newton, who didn't realize that he had just made a sensational observation of gravitational force that would revolutionize the world of science forever.

Later in history, a twenty-eight-year-old, hitherto unknown young man in 1907, while working in a patent office was suddenly struck with an idea, "If a man falls freely, he would not feel his own weight." He later described it in 1922 as his "Eureka moment." This twenty-eight-year-old was none other than Albert Einstein. Physics would never be the same again.

In 1929, Edwin Hubble stunningly discovered the red shift phenomenon that led to the discovery that the Universe was expanding rather than static, as previously thought. This was his Eureka moment. Astronomy took a giant step with this discovery.

We all grew up reading fascinating stories, many in which accidental discoveries changed the course of history and science.

Turn back the pages of history and there are never-ending accounts of such stories.

Though it was not at that level of the events previously mentioned, I had my own Eureka moment as the discussion over the new deadly virus disease was raging all over the world in 2020.

I was working on a particularly busy day and had seen a lot of sick COVID patients that day. As I was looking at the Lab results of a COVID patient, I saw an elevated D-Dimers level. D-Dimer is a test that doctors order when they are suspecting a blood clot somewhere in the body. If the level is below the normal range, then it rules out any clot in the body, be it in lungs, legs or anywhere else. But if it is higher-than-normal range, then it warrants further testing to search for a clot. Those were early days and truly little data was available at that time on the pathogenesis of the deadly virus. Out of blue it just struck my mind that if this virus principally affects the lungs, then it is quite possible that it causes clots in lungs which block the blood flow in areas vital to oxygen exchange. The next thing I did was order a scan of the patient's lungs, and guess what? There were multiple clots on both lungs which is a bit unusual as clots normally originate in one place, usually in the legs where they travel to the lungs and stay on one side. Finding multiple clots on both sides indicated a common generalized source, which could be the virus. It was a sensational discovery, as there were no previous accounts of clots in any available reports listed as one of the main reasons for breathing issues in COVID patients.

It was a Eureka moment for me, and I started ordering D-Dimers Test on patients who suffered with respiratory issues. I consistently found widespread occurrences of these clots, and started ordering prophylactic heparin for these patients to prevent clot formation.

I was so overwhelmed with these startling findings that I urgently called the Center for Disease control (CDC) on April 4th, 2020, to record my findings and I shared the information on my Facebook account, which is still there. I didn't have the time or resources to organize a formal study as I was working in a community hospital.

Later it became increasingly clear that this virus causes a hypercoagulable state (making blood thicker) leading to clot formation, especially in lungs.

All over the world, an intense search was in progress to discover the pathogenesis of the disease (How the virus brings about this level of destruction) before a treatment strategy could be worked out.

A Eureka moment didn't occur only once in all of this time since the year 246 BC, it kept striking the minds of generations after generations. Eureka moments hit everyone, and when they strike, all you need to do is to seize the moment and the world is yours.

When you are groping in the dark you sometimes don't realize who will come forward to show you the light and crack the code, and guess who came this time to unfold the riddle?

Dead Men Tell Tales

...when the living ones were dumbfounded, the fallen ones came up to narrate the stories.

17

— • —

"Mortui non morden."

It is an idiom in Latin, and it means "dead men don't bite" and it means killing the enemy is a surefire way to make sure that enemy will not be able to tell what exactly happened. This idiom also means, "dead men tell no tales."

Time and again this phrase comes up in literature, but the first documented use appears to be by Plutarch in Part III of "Life of Pompey," covering the return of Pompey to Rome somewhere from 62 to 48 BC, during the reign of Julius Caesar

(13 July 100 BC – 15 March 44 BC). Plutarch identified Theodotus of Chios as the mastermind behind Pompey's death with the basic idea of removing an enemy so that there would be no reason to fear that enemy anymore as "dead men cannot bite, and dead men tell no tales." Plutarch

was a Greek Middle Platonist Philosopher and historian who lived from 46 AD to 119 AD. He is regarded as the originator of the idiom.

Literature research also reveals the use of this phrase over and over again, be it published in *The Star and Sentinel Newspaper* (1882) as "Friend of Garfield," or in *Porcupine's Gazette* by William Corbett (1797), or by John Dryden in *The Spanish Fryar* in 1681, or in *The Dead Men and Tales* by Thomas Beacon in 1560, or by *Sheikh Sadi* of Shiraz in 1250.

I could talk about this for hours, but this idiom basically means silencing your enemies so that they cannot reveal your secrets. But if that was the intention of the deadly corona, then it didn't provide any service to the king. It killed its victims ruthlessly with lightning speed, but their stories were not to be buried so easily.

In fact, Dead men have been telling tales for a long time. The forensic examination of the dead bodies reveals a lot about the circumstances in which death occurred. Dissections of the cadavers by Henry Gray opened the whole knowledge of Anatomy.

As corona deaths were climbing during the pandemic, bio-scientists wasted no time in starting to do postmortem studies on the persons who died of the deadly infection.

Ruins can sometimes reveal not only what the level of destruction was, but also the nature of the destruction.

It is not my intension to go into technical details or medical jargon, but I will highlight some of the important findings that were made during autopsies and their relevance to improved medical management following those discoveries.

It was found that brunt of the damage was taken on by the lungs. This was not surprising as the disease primarily presented with breathing issues. Essentially the virus was found in every organ, which showed the stunning ability of the virus to enter any organ. Cells have an area on their outer membranes which is called, in medical terminology, the ACE-2 receptor and it is present on virtually every body cell. The virus had the ability to bind to it and it virtually served as a gate pass for the virus to enter the cell, take control of cellular biochemical machinery, and use it to its own advantage to produce millions, billions and trillions of copies of itself (replication). It was essential to survival of the virus, but it came at the cost of the health of its human host. The virus virtually believed in the dictum: "If one of us has to die, then it better be you first!"

Windpipes of lungs (trachea, bronchi) are like an inverted tree and at their ends are air bubble-like, thin-walled structures called alveoli where gas exchange primarily happens. Alveoli were found to be diffusely damaged and filled with exudative fluids in the form of a membrane, which was preventing gas exchange and hence causing low oxygen levels available to body tissues required for many vital biochemical processes in cells. In such situations the body normally responds by stimulating respiration in an effort to improve oxygenation and air hunger (shortness of breath) develops.

They also found that there were micro-thrombi (small clots) in blood vessels in virtually every organ, especially the lungs, heart, kidneys, spleen, lymph nodes, and liver. These were interfering with the nutrition of the organs and system specific manifestations developed.

The cells of the heart muscle, brain, kidney, and liver became swollen and started to degenerate. Internal bleeding into the spleen, liver and other organs was damaging these organs. Multiorgan damage was obvious. Breathing was compromised from lung damage, and patients had suffered from altered mental status from brain cell swelling. The heart muscle enzyme (Troponin) leaked into the blood stream due to heart muscle inflammation (myocarditis), kidney failure was caused by cellular damage, diarrhea resulted from gastrointestinal cellular inflammation and damage, and liver failure occurred due to liver cell swelling and damage, to name a few.

Autopsy results started to pour in and the best brains in the world started to revise their strategies for medical management.

The autopsy studies led to the rapid adoption of new policies like the usage of blood thinning agents to prevent clots before they happened, aggressive rehydration, revised strategy of ventilators to improve oxygenation of lungs and to avoid barotrauma of the lungs, the use of antibiotics in superimposed secondary infections, and switching nebulizers to inhalers to avoid dissemination.

Autopsy investigators found charred, burned, scarred organs, and structures reminiscent of a ruthless invading army leaving behind the ruins. The unfortunate victims did their job, but it was up to the scientists now to learn from the autopsy findings and take the fight back to the king.

The next question we faced was, which weapons did the king's armies possess that caused such devastation?

Did the king possess weapons of mass destruction?

"Weapons of Mass Destruction"

The king resorts to the dictum: Use your weakness to your own advantage to win a battle.

18

One of my childhood stories told about a giant elephant who was killed by a small ant. I always wondered how that could be.

"Cinco de mayo" is celebrated on every fifth of May, more so in the USA than in Mexico itself, to celebrate Mexico's victory over the Second French Empire at the Battle of Puebla in 1862. It was led by Mexican general Ignacio Zaragoza who used his knowledge of local geography and his clever tactics to improvise and defeat a much larger, better equipped, superior army.

In history there are innumerable accounts of weaker opponents defeating more powerful ones. How did corona do it?

Coronavirus is an RNA virus that doesn't have its own DNA, and so it requires someone else's

DNA to produce its own ingredients which are vital for its replication and propagation, and hence its own survival. Sounds like a weaker dependent creature! In fact, its weakness is its biggest weapon as it has the intelligence to use it to its own advantage and it did not matter to the King if the one that helped it propagate suffered badly or died. All is fair in love and war, isn't it?

The bio–lab that corona is looking to generate its multiples is located inside the cell. It attaches to an area over the surface of the cell called the ACE2 receptor, and enters the cell where it uses its replicase gene to recruit host cell enzymes and amino acids to produce its own replicas and virions, which in turn are carried to the cell's surface and released to the exterior to enter other cells where this cycle is repeated somewhat akin to nuclear fusion in a reactor. In this fashion, new baby coronas are produced to be released for infecting other cells. Eventually the bodily resources of nutrients are used up, leading to the demise of the host. By this time, progeny viruses have gained access to the secretions, especially the lungs, and are breathed out to seek other hosts. Completely **overwhelming bodily nutrients** is one of the weapons that the virus uses for its own survival to the detriment of its host.

Dissemination to all parts of body is widespread as ACE2 receptors are virtually located on all organs, which leads to **multiorgan failure**.

Cellular and organ damage is also caused by small blood clots called **Microthrombi** that develop in virtually every organ and severely jeopardize the blood supply and hence compromise the nutrient and oxygen supplies. Clots can break and be carried away in circulation (a process called **thromboembolism**) which can become lodged in vital organs like the lungs or the brain and cause damage to these organs by interrupting their blood supply.

Local tissue damage will provoke an inflammatory response from the body which is protective and aims to limit the infection to the area where it started. Such enzymes and chemicals released are called Cytokines, and these escape into the bloodstream, which carries them all over. This is called a **Cytokine Storm**. It has its own deleterious effects, including dilatation of blood vessels which causes more swelling in organs and generalized fevers, hence the name "pyrogens which in common language means fever producing chemicals. It caused more damage in lungs than in other organs, and the lungs were already compromised in their ability to oxygenate, so they became flooded with fluids. Early attempts by doctors to remedy this was to forcibly induce oxygenation in the lungs by selecting High pressures called **PEEP** (Positive End Expiratory Pressure) on ventilators (breathing machine in ICU). This turned out to be more deleterious as it caused further trauma inside lungs from high pressure. It is known as **Barotrauma**.

Swelling, stagnation of fluids, and loss of fluid into tissues (called third spacing in Medicine) led to **Dehydration** that compromised the overall hydration status and supply of water to vital organs, further compromising their functions. Sequestration and stagnation of secretions led to growth of bacteria causing additional infection in addition to the virus itself, which is termed **secondary bacterial infection**.

I could go on forever about it, but that is for the healthcare professionals to deal with. My intention is to give the readers some idea of what armamentarium was at the disposal of the virus to bring about destruction of this magnitude.

So, now I do believe the story that an Ant killed the Elephant, and it did so by entering through elephant's trunk, causing widespread damage inside while the giant elephant struggled violently and helplessly, all in vain. What a clever tactic by the ant against a vastly superior enemy who could literally kill it simply by stepping on it.

There is an old dictum, "There is no such thing as a small enemy." Neither was our King corona. Its size might be small, but it greatly outsmarted us in wisdom and greatly outnumbered us in population size and it did this by using our bodily resources for its own propagation.

But who would stop this onslaught? Hopes rose and fell rapidly as many so-called promising agents did not live up to the initial claims, and we aimlessly faced the broken promises. So, the biggest question we faced was, who will "bell the cat?"

BROKEN PROMISES

*...when adversity prevails, hopes rise with each promise
but when promises break, hopes dwindle!*

19

Someone told me a while ago that both promises and rules are made to be broken. It's a shocking statement. So, who can you trust then?

The ruthless king's armies were on a rampage, slaying everyone that came their way. With our backs to the wall, we kept on fighting without any effective strategy with promises of fresh and new ammunition on its way to us. Rumors were rife. There was not enough time to authenticate the weaponry supplied to us. It reminded me of the guerilla war for the independence of Mexico when people even used kitchen utensils to fight. Similarly, the onus was on us as we were the guardians of health and life.

It was hard.

We started weekly ad hoc meetings with infectious disease specialists and pharmacies to review the latest recommendations for medications that could manage and control the new disease. We were vehemently reviewing literature, news from research papers, the CDC, WHO, newspapers, media, on a minute-by-minute basis. Most of these proved to be no more than a mirage in the burning desert.

One of the first medications that was handed out to us was **Hydroxychloroquine/chloroquine** (Quinine). It began as an experimental treatment for COVID in China because of its previously known antiviral, anti-inflammatory, and immuno-modulatory properties. There was high excitement about it. In some developing countries, Chloroquine disappeared from the market as retailers wanted to exploit the demand, however, it was available here in the USA. It turned out to be futile and in fact it was found to have serious side effects, including Gastrointestinal upsets and damaging effects on the hearts of some individuals. It rapidly lost its charm and was withdrawn from the treatment options.

News started to pour in from Italy suggesting the beneficial effects of **vitamin D** because studies on affected individuals showed widespread low vitamin D levels. Also, there were suggestions about the usage of **Zinc**. Then came news of **Ivermectin** (medication for worms) through word of mouth, without any endorsement from studies or CDC or FDA. These quickly lost interest as there were no observed benefits.

As time went by, somewhat better medications and treatment strategies started to emerge, but there was still no real breakthrough.

Soon an injection called **Tocilizumab** came out on the market, and was developed based on the observation that it targeted and dampened the gush of inflammatory enzymes and chemicals called "Cytokine Storm" that caused more damage than the virus itself. The results were equivocal, and it was too early to draw conclusions. It was reserved for ventilated patients who could not be taken off ventilators. The results were not as encouraging as you would hope for in such dire circumstances.

Ventilators were viewed as the gold standard for respiratory ailments, but once COVID patients got ventilated, only twenty percent survived. The health industry was not keeping pace with the supply of new ventilators. The severe shortage of ventilators was hitting the national news. Complications with ventilators were being increasingly reported. Very high pressures were being used (called **PEEP: positive end expiratory pressure**) and it caused damage to lungs (Barotrauma) and was having no effect on survival. Later it turned out to be the wrong strategy.

Another treatment that came out was **COVID Plasma,** which was harvested from COVID survivors' blood on the basis that if they survived then they must have procured, due to their immune system, protective antibodies against COVID in them. Results were equivocal and no survival benefit was observed.

Amidst the chaos and futile attempts at finding a magic drug, the fight against COVID continued despite these failures. We were waiting for the silver lining.

When would the clouds part for a ray of hope to sneak through?

Silver Lining in the Clouds

...when it all looked like a lost battle, some new arms arrived for the beaten and bruised warriors to equip them.

20

— • —

....and out of the haze a stunning knight on horseback suddenly appeared in shining armor, riding on a white unicorn with flying colors and blinding lights, he pulled his glistening sword out and rescued the most beautiful golden-haired princess in the whole world, and took her to the magic land with stars, flowers, colors, lights, green meadows, sky kissing mountains, floating clouds, blue streams singing their way down the rocks, and they lived happily ever after....

We were waiting for an ending like that, but unfortunately a happy ending remained elusive despite all our efforts. We struggled with rumors of magic medications descending on us from heavens. They proved futile and one after another got discarded.

A few bright spots started to crop up here and there. A company announced that it was developing **neutralizing antibodies,** which would occupy the receptor site on the cells where virus enters the cell interior. This would block the propagation of viruses. It never materialized in time, but the research continued across the globe.

A much brighter revelation was the development of a drug named **Remdesivir.** Its mode of action was to insert itself into the multiplying virus strands and terminate its maturation. It was relatively encouraging news, but while it shortened the hospital stay in the trials, it didn't confer the mortality benefit. It also caused bad effects on the liver.

However, it was widely adopted into management of COVID patients. Long-term benefits and effectiveness were too early to be deduced. While availability and cost were issues in many parts of the world, insurance companies generally accepted it here in the USA.

By this time, it was clear that **Chloroquine, Vitamin D, Zinc, Ivermectin** had no role to play in the management and were withdrawn from the management plans.

The BCG vaccination is normally administered to guard against tuberculosis and was proposed to increase the general immunity and hence enhance body's overall ability to fight the viral disease better. It was extensively used in Europe but no independent confirmation could be obtained, and it didn't gain popularity in the USA.

Social distancing, mask mandate, and hand hygiene remained in place and appeared to be the most effective tools.

As it became increasingly clear that the high **PEEP pressures** of ventilators were causing more damage, prompt extensive revision of ventilator management was carried out and adoption of reduced PEEP pressures had a beneficial outcome.

Prophylactic anticoagulation had a good impact on the prevention of widespread clots and helped to decrease mortality rates. Some markers like **ferritin levels, D-Dimers, and C-reactive protein**, for detection of severity of inflammation and cytokine storm were identified to be very useful. These were checked through blood tests. They proved to be useful in taking prompt action and making critical decisions in management.

The use of **antibiotics** like azithromycin and Levaquin was started to address the secondary bacterial or superimposed bacterial infections experienced by some patients.

The major hope rested on the development of **Herd Immunity.** What this means is that once more than half of the population gets infected, natural immunity will develop in those individuals which will have a protective effect on the rest of the population.

It was a difficult way to stop the propagation of the disease, and we wondered if it was the only way to create immunity. Obviously, we needed a vaccine, but it was still elusive.

Then, out of the blue a study emerged from Oxford which brought to light a time-honored simple medicine that happened to be cheap as well. It was announced that **steroids** at a low dose seemed to be reducing mortality rates in COVID patients. The moment the news broke out, it was promptly and extensively adopted across the world. It was the first time any medication had been shown to reduce mortality in trials. It was indeed a silver lining in the clouds.

With better ventilator management, improved PPE, and the arrival of steroids, the outlook appeared much better than before.

The background work was underway and intense research was going on behind the scenes, though pharmaceutical companies were reluctant to share the results at distinct phases of trials for obvious reasons.

The magic moment still had not come, but hope was there. There was a gut feeling that from somewhere a rescue ship would appear and save humanity from the brink of disaster.

The stage was set for Armageddon and a final war between good and the evil at what seemed like the end of the world was about to unfold!

Turbulence in Ether

*When the emotional journey began to feel less bumpy,
the demon reared its ugly head yet again.*

21

In the 19th century, an imaginary substance was believed to be filling the vast space in the universe between heavenly bodies. It was named "ether," also known as "aether" or "luminous ether." Scientists, including big names like Isaac Newton, believed it was the medium through which electromagnetic waves are transmitted. On a lighter note, I could imagine teenage lovers of those times saying, "I will send my love to you through the ether, wherever you might be." The waves travelling through the ether were imagined to cause ripples. Space was not believed to be as vast as it is perceived to be now.

Whenever I go down memory lane and think of COVID times in 2020, it feels as if we were floating aimlessly in the ether, and wave after wave was hitting us like ripples while the eddies and turbulence swirled us around and around. As we were cruising through time, tides of COVID were about to hit us one after the other.

What would life be like if you were to be on a roller coaster forever? You would go up and suddenly drop down, feeling it was the end of the world, but you would survive and just when you would feel it's over, the worst would hit you again, and yet again. Then there is the feeling of uncertainty, that it will never end.

In the medical field, we seriously believed at that time that the rest of our lives were going to be like this. We thought we would perpetually be socially distancing and wearing masks. The media was presenting a horrific picture of the situation, but at the same time reminding everyone that even the Spanish Flu, after wreaking havoc for two years, suddenly calmed down.

It became a way of life to survive those torrid times. We had accepted that we didn't have an effective medicine available to kill the virus, but some new management strategies had emerged as to how best help the victims and protect our own survival. Some emerging medications and treatments had partial responses only.

Warnings of a second wave were already coming shortly after the first one. In China, a new outbreak was detected on June 11, 2020, while running an aggressive campaign of COVID testing around the Xinfadi Wholesale Food Market in the southwestern Fengtai district. This happened after a run of fifty-six days without reports of any new local infections. It was a clear indication that it wasn't over yet.

In the USA, the officially reported death toll crossed 100,000 in May 2020, but as a general consensus, in the medical community the actual number was significantly higher than that. This was based on the fact that testing was not universally available to all because of limited supply of test kits and many remote areas were just ignored. Some people didn't have the resources to even make it to hospital or even get tested. Collection of data had its bias, which even WHO and CDC acknowledged.

A second wave was reported in July and August of 2020. In November 2020 a third wave was reported which peaked during December 2020 and beyond. The death toll was nearing half a million in USA alone, as per official reports but most likely grossly underestimated.

This highlighted the inadequacy of management strategies. A race against time was underway.

By December 2020, we had come a long way. We had embarked on an unbelievable journey of hard work, uncertainty, sacrifices, self-belief and above all, perseverance.

The battle-hardened warriors of medicine were ready for any eventuality, even self-annihilation.

THE TAMING OF THE SHREW

...Shakespeare busted the myth of how to tame the shrew, but what do you do when you are up against an unseen shrew?

22

Between 1590-1592 AD, the famous playwright William Shakespeare wrote a comedy in which Petruchio tames a headstrong, obdurate Katherina who is depicted as a shrew. A shrew is a small mammal who is very territorial and unsociable, and thirteenth century superstitions associated with this animal led people to use the word shrew to describe a stubborn, ill-mannered person. A similar story line has been traced back to *Arabian Nights* and has been featured in many movies. That's a brief history of this theme. Nearly everyone comes across some kind of shrew in their own life. Not all of them can be tamed though, I can confirm.

How do you tame a shrew who is a problem for all of humanity, and not just you personally? Tough, isn't it?

It was tough indeed, especially when it took a toll on human life, and not just human comfort, as in other stories of the shrew.

Time is the best teacher and it's the essential ingredient in taming any shrew, along with sheer endurance.

To tame the coronavirus, we worked out a strategic plan. First, we needed to identify those who were infected.

Viral Testing came quickly to the fore, but it took a couple of days to get back a result. Initial false negatives were high, up to about fifty-four percent (PMC PubMed Central). This led to unnecessary quarantine until test results became available.

Eventually **Rapid testing** became available, though false negatives were even higher.

The next step was to **quarantine** those who tested positive to limit the transmission. This had its own issues as not everyone had places at home where they could isolate themselves and still be looked after by family members without spreading the infection. Some people with small children simply couldn't afford to do it.

Next was **contact tracing** to limit the spread. Widespread viral testing was laborious and not always possible.

Hospitalization was still unavoidable in severely affected patients, especially those with breathing issues.

Negative Pressure Isolation Rooms were still required, as we entered the relapse phase, but were not easily available due to the immense disease burden in the community.

To estimate the level of immunity in the individuals and in the community, **an antibody test** was needed. On September 23, 2020, the US Food and Drug Administration issued an emergency use authorization (EUA) for the first serology (antibody) point-of-care (POC) test for COVID-19 (FDA NEWS RELEASE on September 23, 2020).

Medications which showed some promise like Steroids, Heparin, Remdesivir had widely been adopted towards the end of 2020 to reduce severity of the disease, with some variable success.

Raising the General public awareness did help but as always happens, many were reluctant to cooperate for personal reasons.

Disinfectants, gloves, masks, social distancing, and quarantine continued to be in widespread use though reports of violation were also coming here and there.

Border controls and testing on visitors from highly infected areas continued to be employed with variable success.

A seesaw amplitude of control of the spread, versus lapses in following policy were widely observed. All of the aforementioned measures were effective to some extent, but none of them were perfect. Human nature played a big role.

Rays of hope overwhelmed the sense of loss and we dreamt of a new dawn where we would rise from the depths of despair and achieve a long-awaited victory.

ARMAGEDDON

...a final standoff between good and the evil as

the humans' last-ditch efforts stood against the invis-ible enemy.

23

The destination was far, the path was rough and uncertain, the darkness surrounded us, the weather was stormy, and there wasn't even a faint glimmer of light to show the way. Worn-out mates were falling to the wayside, and amidst that gloominess we just burned the candle of our hearts and slowly inched towards apocalypse. An apocalypse in the form of destruction of the world as we knew it was staring us in the face. Still, we held onto hope.

As we entered the last few weeks of December 2020, a final war was imminent, and everyone waited for the final punch from God. We strolled, we stumbled, we regrouped and struggled to rise to its feet.

Battle-hardened warriors were still putting up a ferocious resistance.

We had come a long way by the end of 2020. A year of gigantic challenges, a year of uncertainty, a year of struggle, heroism, resistance, losses, hopes, setbacks, and sacrifices.

The silent work that had been going on behind the scenes to develop a vaccine to prevent the virus from propagating through the body deeply affected individuals and anticipation was felt in each community.

Behind the scenes, efforts and intense research work remained shrouded in mystery as tight-lipped pharmaceutical companies wouldn't budge into releasing early results or share the harmful side effects of the vaccine on volunteers. This was for an obvious reason, as they didn't want a bad reputation before the vaccine was rolled out to public.

Still, this was contrary to a long-standing doctrine of American Law:

"Caveat Emptor"

In simpler terms, it means "Let the buyer know," or, "The buyer alone is responsible for checking the quality and suitability of the goods before the purchase."

News was emerging that China had developed a vaccine that was authorized for emergency use in China and was first administered on July 22, 2020. It was called the Sinopharm BIBP vaccine (BBIBP-CorV). Months before its release, Chinese authorities had already lifted their lockdown restrictions. The results of the new vaccine were not available for a while.

In August of 2020, Russia had registered a COVID-19 vaccine called Sputnik.

These vaccines didn't gain popularity in the West, where scientists were developing their own vaccines.

By December 2020, two breakthrough vaccines were announced. One was from Pfizer and the other one was from Moderna. It was astonishing that we had developed vaccines in just under a year's time frame. During the second half of December 2020, these two vaccines were rolled out to hospitals and were administered to a select population of high-risk citizens.

The development of vaccines has been one of modern Medicine's greatest achievements. Turning back the pages of history to May 1796, a physician from Berkley, United Kingdom, named Edward Jenner inoculated an eight-year-old named James Phipps with matter collected from another person who had cowpox sore. History was made. The world of Immunology exploded into existence. Jenner had made observations that people who were infected with cowpox never developed smallpox which was a much deadlier disease. He believed some changes happened in the body after experiencing the milder disease of cowpox, which protected the person from contracting the more deadly smallpox disease. It proved to be one of the greatest discoveries of all time and kick-started the science of Immunology while saving millions of lives across the globe.

Mankind never looked back. Vaccines came to the rescue of mankind again and again and in my career as a doctor, they fought against one the deadliest pandemics I had ever lived through.

There was widespread enthusiasm and public interest to receive the vaccine one way or the other. Though, as always happens, some people remained skeptical and reluctant to get vaccinated.

News was breaking that the final punch we were waiting for against the virus had arrived. Obviously, time was crucial in judging its full effectiveness and establishing a side effects profile.

In the dwindling days of 2020, we felt the ammunition we had been lacking against the Corona virus had finally been delivered to us.

Hope was restored and a sense of victory was in the air. As we looked to the new year ahead, we had a feeling that finally we got the better of king corona, but questions still haunted us. Was this the final victory? Was our struggle with the virus over? Was this the Armageddon we were looking for, when the final victory of good over evil would be achieved? Finally, the fog had started to clear, and glittering rays of hope started to break through the dark clouds.

ETERNAL FIRE AND THE KING

...a fire in the belly can cool down even the most ferocious fires of the world.

24

I grew up reading about Homer and the story of the blind Greek poet always fascinated me, like millions of others. As a blind bard singing in the streets of ancient Greece, Homer lived around the eighth century BC. He left indelible marks on the pages of history that stood the test of time. He is credited as the author of two Epic poems, *The Iliad,* and *The Odyssey*. He may have created many more works, but only these have survived the test of time. Whether he wrote them, or they were transferred from him by word of mouth is unknown, but his influence on history is incredible.

In his work *The Iliad*, he mentioned, "The fire that never goes out," as he was referring to natural gas springing out of cracks of limestone in a mountainous area located a few miles west of Olympos. This fire has been burning for centuries, and is known as "Chimaira" (burning stone) in the Bellerophontos mythology.

Aristotle ignited the debate by declaring that the universe is composed of four basic elements including fire, earth, water, and air, but he failed to identify which one was the main element. Heraclitus, an ancient pre-Socratic Greek philosopher (540-480 BC) differed from Thales of Miletus, also a pre-Socratic Greek philosopher (626 –548 BC), who claimed everything is made of water, by asserting that fire was the main element.

We have come a long way since that discussion started, but the very nature of these four elements hasn't changed much.

Fire by nature is very explosive, angry, and dramatic, and seems to want to propagate and control everything that surrounds it. Who can deny the power of the fiery globe in the sky, the sun, or the awe of the soothing glow of the stars in the cosmos, who are harboring cataclysmic explosions of fire in them? We only see fire on earth in significantly smaller versions. Fire requires fuel, ignition, and a substrate to keep feeding it. No one understands this better than the early humans, Homo Erectus, who about a million years ago started using fire in a controlled way to their own advantage. Food has certainly become tastier ever since then, I can tell you that!

The eternal fire is the "one that never goes out." Be it the one mentioned in *The Iliad* by Homer, or the burning mountain, Wingen in Australia where fire has been burning for 6,000 years, or even the coal mine fire of Centralia in Pennsylvania, which has been burning beneath the borough since 1962. It needs a constant supply of fuel and a substrate, in all cases.

What relevance does this have with the corona virus? King Corona exploded on the world stage in the last days of 2019. It spread like a fire across the globe and even the waters of Atlantic and Pacific couldn't halt its march. What ignited it? We don't know, just as we don't know what ignited the big bang over 13.8 billion years ago, which led to the birth of the ever-expanding observable universe. King corona wanted to continue to support its eternal fire by feeding on a substrate called humans. Kings always operate like that, don't they? But the substrate it chose this time was the wrong one.

It seemed corona could have gone on relentlessly until it had consumed all of humanity. At least it felt like it in the beginning. The heat and intensity of the King corona's desire for eternity was unbelievable.

A menace is a menace only while you give in to it. The guardian angels of the healthcare field rose to their feet and stood firm in the face of the challenges posed by the virus.

A fire in the belly can cool down any fires of the world. The burning desire of these guardians to save human lives was unmatched. Observing the territories that had fallen to the King, and crossing the rough terrains littered with corpses, the unarmed warriors of healthcare kept marching on. There was always a victory in mind and a self-belief that we would emerge as victors.

As 2020 drew close to an end, there was a gut feeling that a new era would begin in the year ahead. The flames of Hope had never before flickered so high!

What Lies Next?

...and Sam lived to tell the tale.

25

Growing as a young child, I loved to look at the stars glittering up in the dark skies like diamonds in the night. Nothing fascinated me more than talking about the stunning views of faraway worlds, the skies, other galaxies, planets, or the sun and stars. As I mentioned before, my mom, Nargis, was a great storyteller. She used to tell me a bedtime story in which a young boy's dream came true and he flew to a star where soothing blue light emitted from the ground, and nimbus clouds would fly over the sky, kissing mountains, and they would come down over the green valleys and shower them with colored rain. Each time there would be a different color rain pouring out of the rainbow. Singing streams would spiral down the mountain's valleys, and gigantic springs would jet into space and drench the dream boy, who would run through the meadows among the flowers and onto the horizon. We never got to the end of the story as I used to fall asleep, and I never remembered to ask her what happened next, or how the story ended. Perhaps I wanted to live in dreamland and never come out of it. She never did tell me the ending.

Growing out of boyhood, I became more interested in the creation and extent of the universe. It was a stunning idea that everything came into existence out of nothing in a big bang, along with the very fact that the whole universe continues to expand like a child blowing bubbles in a soapy tub of water. Time was an enigma for me, and I wanted to know where the edge of the universe was. With astronomy, I became interested in knowing how life came into being on our earth and I wondered, is there another place where there is life, similar or different from ours on earth?

These questions are quite fascinating, and from time immemorial, no one has ever found the answers. Life became a very important thing for me, but that is not the reason I chose medicine as my career. I had to become a doctor as my parents always told me that I would be a doctor, and so I did just that.

I learnt medicine in medical college and the training was centered on how to be tough but compassionate during medical emergencies. It never, ever occurred to me that in my lifetime I would be faced with a situation like being in the middle of a real pandemic, where I would be obligated to not only save others, but also protect myself. It feels like a great absorbing story when you read about the Spanish flu, the Black death, or malaria killing half of the world, but living through such a situation in real life is entirely different. Yes, I was there, right at ground zero where we took the ruthless King corona by the horns with bare hands, and with our backs to wall with no apparent end in sight.

It was hard, but looking back I feel a sense of pride that overshadows the pain of lost companions, sleepless nights, and the fear that came from the demon of uncertainty that reared its head. We did fight, we didn't give up, and at the end of the day the victory falls into the lap of those who believe they are the winners.

There were a lot of lost opportunities, but positives kept coming up. It was the first time I saw the world united against a single enemy and witnessed collective acts of heroism and sacrifice.

All differences were put aside, and a sense of unity swept across the earth. Why shouldn't we live like that forever? In harmony and peace with love and sanity! The King attacked us ruthlessly but left behind a lot of burning questions. After being beaten and bruised, humanity is still licking its wounds, but have the right conclusions been drawn? A battle is never lost until it's lost in your own mind. Today's mighty may be the fallen losers of tomorrow. There is a lot to learn, but the river of time flows relentlessly and one day this will be talked about as "another deadly pandemic that once happened." Mothers will tell stories and another young Sam will become fascinated somewhere in the world.

Sitting in the comfort of my own home and writing these last few words, as I look through the window, I see a beautiful evening coming to an end. Birds are returning home, and a cool breeze is blowing across the meadows, gently stroking the blossoming flowers along the small brook streaming through my backyard. The flowers sprinkle colors all over, and the colors merge with the red horizon. As the darkness descends on the peaks and valleys of Rhode Island, I am not sure what lies next for me or what is lurking out there in the dark, but one thing is for sure; I am ready for another Ground Zero if I stumble upon it yet again.

—Sam Naqvi, MD

REFERENCES

1. President's Speech
    NY Times March 11, 2020.
    National archives Sep 28, 2020

2. Dr. Fauci's Testimony
    CDC Washington March 11,2020.
    Witness Robert R Redfield, MD

3. WHO Announcement
    WHO Director General remarks,
    March,11, 2020

4. Dow Jones Shares
    https://www.statistics.com
    Published by Statista Research Department

5. Randy Gobert tests positive
    Bleacher report by Timothy RAPP,
    March 11,2020.

6. First case of Corona
    Dr. Li Wenliang in chat group on Dec 30,2019
    JNM (Journal of Nuclear medicine)

7. NY cases (March to May)
    CDC "Morbidity & Mortality Weekly report (MMWR)

8. Official death Toll
   CDC official website

9. Leonhard Euler Topology
   Encyclopedia "Brittanica"

10. Spanish Flu
    Wikipedia

11. Diamond Princess Ship report
    Wikipedia

12. Tenerife Hotel report
    Sky News "Travel agent central"

13. Pandemic in Italy
    National Library of Medicine (Pub Med Central)

14. Lockdown in Lombardy
    The Guardian; Wikipedia
    March 8,2020

15. Europe declared Epicenter
    WHO March 11,2020.
    Pub Med Central/National Library of Medicine

16. Italian Docter dies
    Euronews.com/Next

17. Belgium/Hungary/UK affected
    Euronews.com/Next

18. April 2020 Global Cases
    WHO

19. China eases lockdown
    Associated Press (AP),
    March 2020

20. First death in USA
    CDC report February 29, 2020
    (Washington Seattle)

21. Brazil becomes epicenter
    Wikipedia

22. First lockdown in Kerala
    Wikipedia (India)

23. Malthus Theory
    Encyclopedia Brittanica

24. Baron George Cuvier
    Wikipedia

25. Triassic Period
    Encyclopedia Brittanica

26. Healthcare worker deaths
    Amnesty International report
    July 13,2020
    European Public Service Union

27. Egyptian Doctor Reprimand
    "The Guardian", July 15,2020

28. COVID Tests
   Pub Med Central (PMC) National Library of Medicine
   PLOS one 2020: 15(12):0242958
   Published online Dec 10,2020
   PMCID: PMC7728293/PMCID.33301459

29. First Chinese vaccine Wikipedia

30. First Russian vaccine Sputnik Wikipedia

31. Edward Jenner First Vaccine
   Mayo Clinic: History of smallpox